TRANCE

TRANCE

K.L. DENMAN

orca soundings

ORCA BOOK PUBLISHERS

Published in Canada and the United States in 2025 by Orca Book Publishers.
orcabook.com

Library and Archives Canada Cataloguing in Publication
Title: Trance / KL Denman.
Names: Denman, K. L., 1957- author
Series: Orca soundings.
Description: Series statement: Orca soundings
Identifiers: Canadiana (print) 20240453433 | Canadiana (ebook) 20240453441 |
ISBN 9781459841321 (softcover) | ISBN 9781459841338 (PDF) |
ISBN 9781459841345 (EPUB)
Subjects: LCGFT: Novels.
Classification: LCC PS8607.E64 T73 2025 | DDC jC813/.6—dc23

Library of Congress Control Number: 2024943896

Summary: In this high-interest accessible novel for teen readers, Kira races against the clock to find a way to save her friend Brigid, who is trapped in a telepathic trance.

Orca Book Publishers is committed to reducing the consumption of nonrenewable resources in the production of our books. We make every effort to use materials that support a sustainable future.

Orca Book Publishers gratefully acknowledges the support for its publishing programs provided by the following agencies: the Government of Canada, the Canada Council for the Arts and the Province of British Columbia through the BC Arts Council and the Book Publishing Tax Credit.

Design by Ella Collier.
Edited by Gabrielle Prendergast.

Printed and bound in Canada.

28 27 26 25 • 1 2 3 4

For our ancestors. If we go back far enough,

you are shared by us all.

To understand and reconnect with our stories, the stories of the ancestors, is to build our identities.

—author Frank Delaney

Chapter One

It's one of those perfect June days. Warm sun, blue sky, fresh green leaves on the trees. A light breeze carries a sweet scent, and Brigid stops to sniff.

"What a pretty smell."

"Yeah." I look around. "I think it's coming from this shrub."

"Mmm," Brigid agrees. Then she throws me a look. "Please don't bring up one of your apps, Kira. I don't need to know what kind of shrub it is."

I grin and drop my phone back into my bag. "Okay. We do need to keep moving. Laney will be waiting."

Brigid nods, and the charms woven into her half-crown braid tinkle. As usual, she looks like she could have wandered out of an old painting. Brigid doesn't do trendy—she does *her*. She decided a few years ago that her strange talent made normal impossible. We've been besties since fifth grade, when we bonded over our red hair. Hers is bright orange, long and curly. Mine is darker, and I wear it short.

"So what do you know about Laney?" she asks. "Why does she want a reading?"

I retrieve my phone and bring up my Brigid app. "Okay, she's a year younger than us. Just finished tenth grade. Heard about you from another kid at school. Said she wanted a reading because she thinks there's a secret in her family. Something they're not telling her."

"Okay." Brigid nods. "And she has family nearby?"

"Of course." Nearby family is a *must* for what's about to happen. Just in case something goes wrong. "She has an older sister."

"Perfect." Brigid looks ahead, down the street. We're walking along the quiet side of the park, heading for a special bench. It sits in the shade of a large cedar, a tree Brigid loves. She says that trees, with their roots and branches, are her emblem. Maybe even a kind of energy source. She learned they talk to each other through an underground network, and she feels her talent works like that too. "I think Laney's already there."

A girl is sitting on the bench, and as we get closer, she turns to watch us approach. I've never met Laney in person. We just exchanged messages, but this girl looks like the photo she sent. I've asked for photos since the time we started talking to the wrong person. That got weird.

Laney gives us a tiny wave, and when we're close enough, I say, "Hey. Laney?"

"Yes." She stands, and her hands twist nervously. "Brigid?"

"I'm Kira. The one you messaged." I tip my head. "This is Brigid."

Brigid is already doing her thing, gathering herself. It's as if she pulls all her energy inward and holds it there. She offers Laney a quick smile.

Instructions are my job. "Okay, Laney. Here's what's going to happen. You two will sit together, and Brigid will take your hand. It'll take about ten seconds before she's able to connect with one of your ancestors. Then she'll be with them for a while. Could be a few minutes, could be longer. It's usually only around five minutes."

Laney's eyes are huge. "Okay."

Brigid sits and pats the bench beside her. Laney giggles nervously and sits next to Brigid. "Omigod. I'm so excited. I hope it works!"

"It will," I say. "But just a few more things. Laney, once you take Brigid's hand, you might feel some tingling or buzzing. Lately a couple of people also felt as if they went into something like a dream. Whatever happens, you *must* maintain the hold until Brigid comes back. Oh, and sometimes Brigid goes limp. If that happens, just let her lean on you."

"Got it," Laney says. "What about you, Kira? You're going to wait with us, right?"

"For sure," I reply. "I'll be right here. Ready?"

She nods, and Brigid offers her hand to Laney. Laney takes it, and seconds later Brigid is gone. Even after four years, the trance still shocks me. It's sort of like Brigid instantly falls asleep, only more so. It's maybe more like death. The "something" that is Brigid goes away. Her soul, her essence—I don't know the word for it. I should. But whatever it is that makes someone alive and present simply flies away. Gone.

Brigid goes into the past. The first time it happened was when she was thirteen. We were at

Zoe's sleepover party. She'd invited about eight of us over. We were laughing, blasting music, eating junk food. Playing with makeup, taking photos, discussing crushes and whatever. Back then she and I were part of that group.

Anyway, we were all dancing. Brigid tripped and grabbed Zoe's hand. Zoe stopped her from falling, but Brigid collapsed when Zoe let go. We gathered around her. Someone said we should call 9-1-1. But Zoe said it had felt weird holding Brigid's hand, like she had gotten a shock or something, and maybe Brigid had gotten shocked too. I don't know why, but I said maybe she should take Brigid's hand again. And just like that, Brigid was okay.

"What happened?" we asked.

Brigid said, "Whoa, Zoe. Your great-grandma was a badass."

We were all, like, "What are you talking about?" And then she told us. She'd gone to a misty place where she could see Zoe's great-grandmother.

She didn't know how she knew it was her, but she did. And she watched as Zoe's great-grandmother chased off a bear with a big cast-iron pan.

We were all weirded out, and everyone wanted to know if it was true. Zoe didn't know, so we sent her to ask her mom. She went upstairs, and her mom said, yeah, her grandmother had been a cook in a logging camp. A bear had tried to get into the cookhouse, and she went roaring at it with a frying pan.

When Zoe told us that, everyone went wild. We played with Brigid's strange new ability for the next hour. Girl after girl took her hand. She came back with amazing stories. She said sometimes it was like she could fast-forward through lives, stopping to see highlights. We also figured out that if the person let go, Brigid stayed totally senseless. Finally Brigid said she was tired, said she was done. At least, done for that night. Since then...well...a lot has changed.

I check on Brigid and Laney. I'm standing to one side of the bench and see that Brigid's head has dropped onto Laney's shoulder. Laney looks faraway, like she's lost in a daydream.

And then I glimpse something out of the corner of my eye. A truck is hurtling straight toward us.

"Watch out!" I scream.

Too late.

The sound of the truck hitting the bench. Laney's cry cut short. Brigid's body, airborne. These things somehow register, even as I too am hit, thrown backward, gone.

Chapter Two

It's like trying to wake up and not getting there. I hear sounds around me, loud and soft. They don't make sense. I blink and see someone in a uniform running toward me. I try to sit up. Try to remember where I am and why. Something hurts. The person kneels beside me and says, "I'm a paramedic. You've been injured. Lie still."

"What happened?" I ask.

The paramedic looks at me closely. "There was an accident. Do you remember anything about it?"

An accident? "Um. Not really..." But then an image appears. Brigid, airborne. I call out, "Brigid?"

"Easy," the medic says softly.

My head swivels, and I see a blanket draped over something on the ground. I feel cold and start shaking. "Where's Brigid?"

I turn my head. See shards of broken wood. People gathering in clusters, murmuring. I keep looking and glimpse Brigid's red hair fanned out on the grass. Another paramedic kneels beside her. "Brigid!" I try again to sit up. But pain makes me yelp, and I stop.

"What's your name?" the medic asks.

"Kira."

"Okay, Kira, I think you have a broken leg. I'm going to get you stabilized. Then we're going to put you onto a stretcher."

"But what about Brigid?"

He glances at the blanket, then at Brigid. "Is she the other one with red hair?"

"Yes!"

"She's injured too. Unconscious. But don't worry. We're going to get both of you to the hospital. Okay?"

I remember Laney. I look at the blanket on the ground. "What's under that blanket?" I ask.

The medic pats my shoulder. "Don't worry about that right now."

My voice is a whimper. "Where's Laney?"

Another uniform crouches on my other side. Says, "Easy does it, kiddo."

For the first time, I hear sirens. I think I've been hearing them for a while. "Please tell me what happened," I say.

"Don't worry," the medic says in a soothing tone. "Everything will be explained soon. All you need to do is stay still."

I don't stay still. I roll to one side and puke. Some of it gets on the medic. It's impossible to process this. It's like my brain has jammed up. Like it's refusing to go where I want it to go. They put me on the stretcher. Somehow it rises off the ground and rolls right into the back of the ambulance. Another ambulance arrives. Just as the doors close, I see Brigid being wheeled toward it. I try to call out to her. "Brigid?" But even to my ears, my voice is weak.

The next while is a blur. I arrive at the hospital and someone asks for my parents' number. I don't see Brigid or Laney. They give me something for pain, and I drift away. When I wake, I see Mom and Dad. Mom is somber, like always. Dad looks like someone just fried him with a jolt of electricity. His eyes are wild, and his hair is sticking out every which way. My laugh comes out like a weird choking sound.

"Kira!" Dad says. Then: "Nurse! Something's wrong!"

"Dad," I croak. "I'm fine. I was laughing at your hair."

He looks confused. "My hair?" He runs a hand over his head, then squints at me. "They said your head should be fine, but maybe not."

The nurse arrives, checks the monitors. Looks at me and smiles. Says, "Hi, Kira. How are you feeling?"

"Uh..." And then it all comes rushing back. "Where's Brigid? And Laney? Are they okay? What happened?"

Silence.

I look at Mom. "Mom?"

She looks everywhere but at me. Then she touches my hand. "Mom?" I repeat.

She draws a deep breath. Lets it out. "Brigid is in a coma. And the other girl...Laney? I'm sorry, Kira." She shoots me a swift glance.

"Dad?" I fix him with a stare. "What happened to Laney?"

"Sorry, kid. They said...she didn't make it."

I swear, and they just nod. No rebuke for the bad language.

"What happened?"

Mom looks at the floor. Dad shakes his head. "We've heard...that an elderly man had a heart attack at the wheel. Or something. He was probably dead before he hit you girls."

The truck driving straight at us. I see it again and shudder. "God," I whisper. "Oh God. And now Laney is dead. And Brigid..."

A coma? The doctors think she's in a coma. It's not a coma. She's trapped in the trance. In the past.

Chapter Three

I want to run to the doctors and tell them about Brigid. Tell them she's in a trance. Stuck somewhere watching one of Laney's ancestors. And she can't come back unless Laney takes her hand again.

Or a close blood relative of Laney's takes it. We experimented with all this back when it started. A couple of sisters hung out in our group, and if one released Brigid's hand, the other could bring her back. Brigid decided that was a good fail-safe. In case the person freaked out and left or something else happened.

I never thought we'd really need the fail-safe. Now we do. We need someone in Laney's family to take Brigid's hand. But if I tell the doctors that, they won't believe me. They'd probably keep me in the hospital, run tests on my brain. And I need to get out of here.

I look at Mom. "Do you have my phone?"

She frowns. "Your bag is here. I'll check." She reaches down and lifts my favorite purple bag. Rummages inside and pulls out the phone. "Do you want to call someone?"

"No. I just wanted to make sure it's here." On that phone is the special app I coded to keep track of Brigid's readings. All the contact info is there, including Laney's emergency contact number.

Laney. I didn't know her, but what happened to her, to us—I can't process it. "Can we just go home now?"

"Soon," the nurse says. "We have to wait for the doctor to discharge you. But from what she said, it should be fine. Once you've got some crutches, I think you can leave."

Crutches? I look at my leg and see it's wrapped in a cast. It seems distant. Like it doesn't matter. My eyes drift shut.

I wake to the doctor bending over me. "Kira? How are you feeling?" The doctor's face is kind. Concerned. She smiles.

"Uh." My mouth is dry, but I croak, "How is Brigid?"

Her smile fades. "She's still unconscious. We're running tests and will know more soon."

"Is her mother here?" I ask.

The doctor nods. "Yes. How about you? Would you like to go home?"

"Yeah."

"Okay, you got it." She turns to Mom. "That's as long as someone can be with her for the next twenty-four hours. She has a mild concussion, so it's important to watch for symptoms."

“We’ll be there,” Mom says. “What do we need to watch for?”

“Vomiting. Pupils enlarged or uneven in size. Trouble being roused from sleep. Also dizziness or confusion. Vision problems. Any of those may indicate a problem. Kira’s had a shock, so that may affect her too.”

The doctor goes on, about my getting checked again in a week. Mom asks if the family doctor can do that, and she nods. Dad shows up with crutches, and they all help me stand. I’ve never had crutches before, and it seems tricky. They put me in a wheelchair to go to the car, and I notice my shorts are gone. “Where are my shorts?”

Mom says they had to cut them off to work on my leg. *Really?* They drape a sheet over me to get me to the car. Dad says no one will notice. I don’t even care. We drive home in silence. It’s a dull silence. As if there’s a thick blanket of fog over us. They help me inside and straight into my bed.

"Are you hungry?" Mom asks.

I'm not. She sets a small glass of water on the nightstand. And a bell. "Okay. We're going to let you sleep again. We'll keep checking on you, but if you need anything, just ring." She tries to muster a smile.

I'm too tired to smile back. Maybe I nod, then drift away again. I don't know how much time passes. The evening. The night. By morning I want out of bed. I want news of Brigid.

I hobble to the kitchen table, and Dad brings me some toast with peanut butter. I start to eat and am surprised by how hungry I am. It feels wrong to be eating as if nothing has happened. But I'm on my third slice when Mom shows up.

"Mom? Have you talked to Brigid's mom?"

Mom winces. "I tried."

"What did she say? How's Brigid?"

"Kira." Mom sighs. "You know Mrs. Moore. She isn't...friendly. She just said Brigid is in the ICU and no visitors are allowed. And to please not bother her at this time."

Brigid's mother is such a hag. Small wonder Brigid made me swear I'd never breathe a word about her talent around her mom. As if I would.

"No visitors?" I repeat. "For how long?"

"I don't know, Kira," Mom replies. "Usually when someone's in the ICU, it's family only for visitors."

Family only? Brigid's father died when she was two, and she doesn't have any siblings. That means Mrs. Moore is the only one who can tell us what's happening. And I don't trust her.

Chapter Four

Mom talks to the school, and it's agreed that I don't have to return for the final week. My grades are high enough that all my teachers will pass me. Then both Mom and Dad go back to work and I'm left on my own.

A few kids from school reach out to me, ask how I am. I ask them if they've heard about a funeral for Laney. If there is a funeral, I'm going. I've decided it would be better to talk to Laney's sister in person to ask her if she'll go to the hospital. To hold Brigid's hand, bring her back from the shadows. I'll sneak her into the ICU if I have to. Mom calls Mrs. Moore for updates, and when she answers, there's no change. She says the doctors did a CT scan and Brigid has a brain injury. But it doesn't look severe, and they're surprised she hasn't woken up. They are monitoring her.

There's too much time to think. Mostly I think about how the only thing I want is to talk to Brigid. I miss her so much. I think about her "gift." She's done readings for almost four years, for a lot of kids. Told some of them that their ancestors were heroes. One was in a war. Brigid saw him die trying to save another person's life. Other times weren't like that. Like when she gave a reading to Shandy Wilson. Shandy wasn't happy when Brigid told her that her grandfather was a criminal who went to jail. She said Brigid was lying and also was supposed to visit her *heroic* ancestors.

Brigid explained that she had no control over that. She simply went where the talent took her.

And when it became clear that other kids found her strange and were avoiding her? Thought she might put a hex on them or some stupid thing? I said maybe she should stop doing readings.

But she shook her head. "No. It's part of who I am. I don't know why. Maybe I never will. Maybe I'm just a freak of nature. But I'm not going to deny it." Her green eyes got a wicked gleam. "And besides. It's amazing to visit the past. People everywhere and in every time. They're all the same."

I asked what she meant. She said that the things people cared about were the same—love, family, friendship, lust, faith, security. No matter when or where she went, the basics didn't change.

But the readings aren't easy on Brigid. It can take her days to build back her energy. So I suggested she start charging for her time. Weed out those who just wanted a reading for a laugh. Brigid resisted, but when I pointed out she could use the money to save for college or a trip or whatever, she agreed.

"But not expensive," she said. "Only what they can afford, okay?"

Most kids are fine paying her twenty or thirty bucks. For the odd one that can't, Brigid just tells them to pay it forward. Do something for someone else.

Brigid is generous like that.

A memorial service for Laney is announced, stating that all are welcome to attend. It's the day after tomorrow, at a local funeral home. Now I just have to hope Laney's sister will be there. Of course she will.

The day of the memorial, I get up early. I put on my favorite blue dress and call for an Uber to pick me up in plenty of time. I'm slow on the crutches and don't want to be late.

When I arrive, there are people milling around in the lobby. As I hobble in, some of them stare. I hear whispers. "Is that one of the girls from the accident?" I feel eyes following me but don't look at anyone. I'll wait until the service is over before I approach her sister. I don't know what she looks like—maybe like Laney, maybe not. I'm pretty sure the family will sit together up front. I've only gone to one funeral before, when my grandfather died. And we all sat at the front for that.

I choose a seat near the back, and gradually the room fills up. I recognize a few kids from school but don't know them. They're probably Laney's friends. They see me too and come to sit by me.

A girl in pink-framed glasses whispers, "Hey. Kira?"

I nod.

"How did you know Laney?" she asks.

"Uh..."

Music starts playing, and I look toward the front. A group is entering from a side door, walking to take their seats at the front. There are several adults, different ages. A few gray-haired ones, probably grandparents. Everyone is wearing black. One woman is leaning on a man, like she needs him to hold her up.

And yes, a young woman walks beside her too. She doesn't look like Laney, but she must be the sister.

A preacher steps to the front and welcomes us. He says a prayer, and then a slow song starts playing, along with a slide show of Laney. Photos show Laney as a baby, a toddler, a young girl playing soccer. All around me, people start crying.

It looks like a happy life—a life cut short by cruel fate. People step up to the podium to talk about her, and I only hear part of it. My thoughts keep drifting to that moment in the park. That instant of time that changed so much.

And Brigid. Trapped in the past.

Then the young woman with Laney's family stands in front of us. She says, "I remember when my parents adopted Laney..."

And I don't hear anything after that.

Adopted. The word repeats in my head. *Adopted.* I feel dizzy and lean forward. Put my head in my hands.

"Are you okay?" the girl next to me asks.

I shake my head. Take a few deep breaths. Force myself upright. My brain has jammed again, but I need it to work. If Laney was adopted, that means the sister isn't her blood relative. Neither are the parents.

There is no one to save Brigid.

Chapter Five

How could I have been so careless? Me, the person who *always* prepares for the worst, just in case. I like to feel in control of things. So yeah, I asked Laney if she had siblings. She said yes, and that was true. But did I ask her if she was adopted? I've never even thought to ask that question. Why? It seems so obvious now. But in all the readings Brigid has done since we discovered how important it is, we've never needed the blood relative to bring her back. And now, when it's vital...

Nothing else that's said even registers. More music plays, and Laney's family files out. People begin murmuring, standing, leaving.

"Kira?" It's pink-glasses girl again. "I'm Laney's friend Emma. Can we talk to you?"

I focus and find four red-eyed girls crowding around me. "Um. Yeah. But I need the washroom."

She nods. "Okay. We can meet you out front."

I stand, get the crutches in place and slowly make my way to the washroom. I don't really need to go, but if I can dodge the girls, I will. The last thing I need now is talk. The washroom is busy with people splashing water on their faces, blotting tears. I find an open cubicle and go inside. Wait. When voices fade and it seems like everyone is gone, I exit.

Did I wait long enough? I wash my hands and then am trying to open the door when Emma does it for me. "Hey. Thought you might need help." She points at a group of girls. "We're over here."

They turn as one and stare at me. And then I'm surrounded, and questions start flying. "You were there. What happened? How come Laney was with you? What were you doing?"

I stare at them. Surely some of them know why Laney was with me and Brigid. Even though Brigid's gift has been on the down-low, there are rumors. And people like Laney, who hear about it and ask for a reading. "She didn't tell you?"

Emma frowns. "She said she was going to have a surprise. Something about her adoption. I figured she'd found her birth mom. But that wasn't it, was it?" Her stare is accusing. "She went to see your weird friend for a crystal-ball thing, right?"

I nod. "But it's not a crysta–"

"Whatever. Laney is dead because of it." Emma makes it sound like Brigid killed her.

"Yeah. And Brigid's still in a coma," I remind them. "It wasn't her fault. It was the guy that ran over us."

The girls crowd even closer. “But what was Brigid doing to her?”

I don’t have the energy for this. I feel weak. And then another voice cuts in. “Hey. Are you Kira? How are you doing?”

A tall young guy is looking at me. His eyes are red and puffy. I nod, and he steps forward, making the girls give way. He touches my shoulder and says, “I’m Max. A family friend of Laney’s. Looks like you might need to sit down. Come with me.”

There are mutters of protest from the girls, but they step aside. I follow Max, relieved to escape them. He leads me toward a chair in an alcove, tells me to sit. “What can I get for you?” he asks. “There are sandwiches, cake, coffee, tea. Lemonade.”

“I’m fine,” I say.

“You don’t look fine. Wait here. I’ll be right back.” He strides away, and I think about leaving. But before I can muster the strength, he’s back, holding a plate of food. He sets it on the little table beside me, along with a cup of water.

"Thank you," I say. And to be polite, I take a sip of water.

He pulls another chair over and sits. "I'm very sorry for what happened to you and your friend," he says. His eyes are soft with kindness.

"And I'm so, so sorry about Laney," I say. "You said you're a family friend?"

He smiles. Even shaded with sorrow, it's a great smile. A comforting smile. "Our families have been close all my life. Laney was like a cousin to me. Or a little sister even. We grew up together."

A cousin. There could be cousins! I seize on the word until I remember. Any cousin of the family still wouldn't be one to Laney. "Do you know..." I hesitate.

"Do I know what?" he asks.

The words come out in a rush. "Do you know anything about Laney's birth family?"

He shakes his head. "Nope. Why do you ask?"

I shrug. "I just know she was curious about that. She wanted to find out more about them."

"Makes sense," he says. "I'd want to know too. We talked about that sometimes. But it seemed like she had to wait until she was older to get the records. Her parents say they knew nothing about the birth mom. And she wasn't old enough to take a DNA test. Not unless her parents signed her up." He tilts his head. "That's why she was with your friend, wasn't it? A past-life reading or something?"

"Yup."

"And did she get any answers before she died?" he asks.

My head drops. "No."

We're quiet for a few minutes. I want to leave, and remember I need to call for a ride. I dig in my bag and pull out my phone. "Sorry," I say. "I need to call an Uber."

He shakes his head. "Forget that. I'll give you a ride."

"No, it's fine. Thanks, though."

He stands. "Come on. My car is right here, and it's not a problem."

Chapter Six

Max's car is full of weird stuff. There are nets like the type kids use to catch bugs, plastic tubs, other random stuff. He quickly clears the passenger seat, tossing a bag into the back. As I get in, I notice the interior also smells funny.

"Sorry about the mess," he says. "I carry a lot of gear for my summer job."

"What do you do?" I ask.

"I'm working at a nature camp for kids."

"Oh. Cool. So are you, like, catching fish or something?"

There's that smile again. There's even a dimple on one side. "Sometimes. We're more focused on small marine life. Insect larvae and krill that young salmon eat. We're checking to see if there's enough food for the salmon. It's like a science camp. For future environmentalists."

That *is* cool. "Do you like it?"

He nods. "Mostly. It feels good to be working to help nature. But the kids can be a handful. What's your address, Kira?"

I tell him, and on the way he chats more about his work. Tells me that he wants to become an ecologist and the summer job is great experience. The twenty-minute drive goes fast, and when we get to my house, I don't want to go inside. It felt good to have a short break from worry. And I know the worry's going to be even worse now. As in hopeless.

"Is it okay if I call you sometime, Kira?" Max asks. "Just to check in on you?"

"Um. Sure. That would be nice." We exchange numbers. He gets out and comes around to my side of the car. Makes sure I'm all good on the crutches. Watches until I'm at the door. I turn to wave, he raises a hand, and then he's gone.

The next few days are hard. It seems like I'm out of options. I need to talk to someone. But the only one I *could* talk to about this—Brigid—can't be that person. For years we've shared our problems, and even if we didn't solve them, just having each other to talk to made it better.

I search online for ways to find adoption records, but there's no way. Not for me, at least. Mom takes me to the doctor for a checkup, and he says everything seems to be healing.

"My leg itches," I tell him.

He says that's normal.

"How long until the cast comes off?"

He says at least another month. They'll schedule an X-ray to check that the bone has healed. He asks how I'm doing otherwise. Any anxiety? Trouble sleeping?

I shrug.

"She seems to be coping," Mom says. She dislikes oversharing.

The doctor says to come back if I'm having problems. That it's important to pay attention to whole health. Stuff like that.

When we get home, Mom tells me that Brigid's mom hasn't answered her calls for the past couple of days.

"Please keep trying, Mom. I need to know how Brigid is. And if I'm allowed to visit yet."

"We can call the hospital," she replies. "See what they say about it."

She calls and puts it on speaker. The person who answers says Brigid has been moved from the ICU. She's on a regular ward now. Visitors are allowed.

"You mean she's come out of the coma?" Mom asks.

"Let me check." We wait, breath held, for the person to come back on the line. But when she does, she says there's been no change. She can't tell us more than that.

I have to go see her. Mom says she'll take me the next day. Then she heads off to work. But I *need* to see Brigid. Now. Maybe I can take the bus. Problem is, the closest stop is over a block away, and I'm not sure I can handle the distance. I try to convince myself I can. And then a text message pops up on my phone.

Hey. Max here. How are you doing?

Okay, I reply.

Need help with anything?

As it happens, I do. **I hate to ask, but any chance you could drive me to the hospital? I want to visit Brigid.**

No problem. Camp is a half day today. I can be there at about one. That work for you?

Yes! Thank you!

Max shows up right on time. This guy. Could he be any nicer? When I get into his car, it doesn't smell as bad as it did before. I tell him that and am rewarded with his smile.

"I cleaned it out yesterday," he says. "It was getting pretty funky, even for me." He backs the car out of the driveway and asks, "So is there good news about Brigid?"

"I don't know," I reply. "Just heard she's allowed visitors now. But I think she's still in the coma. Whatever's going on, I need to find out."

"For sure. It sounds like she might be improving, though, right?"

"Maybe. I mean, I really hope so. Although—" I stop.

"Although?" He raises a brow.

I almost blurt the truth. That I don't think Brigid can ever "improve" until one of Laney's relatives is found. "Nothing," I mutter.

"Huh. Don't give up hope, Kira. I've heard that people can wake from comas after months. Even years."

"Yeah. From *comas.*" Damn, I shouldn't have said that. Max is too easy to talk to. And I'm desperate to tell someone the truth. Except I know how crazy it will sound, and I don't want him to think I'm crazy.

He looks puzzled, but he doesn't ask more questions. He puts on some music I've never heard. It's nice, just acoustic guitars. I relax into my seat and steal a sideways look at him. "How are Laney's parents?"

"Not good," he says. "They're heartbroken."

"And you?"

He shrugs. "Still find it hard to believe, you know?"

"Yeah."

When we get to the hospital, he says he'll walk in with me but won't go into Brigid's room. He'll give us privacy. Which is perfect. I need time alone with Brigid. There are things I want to say to her. I know from the past that she can sometimes hear while in the trance. Not much, but she once heard me calling her. She'd been gone for almost an hour, and I got worried. I called Brigid's name. It didn't bring her out of the trance. But afterward she said she had heard me. She said my voice was very faint and far away, but she'd heard.

I hope she hears me now.

Chapter Seven

Brigid looks small and pale in the hospital bed. Her hair has been pulled into a single braid, vivid orange on the white pillow. A tube runs from her nose to a bag of liquid hanging overhead. A needle is taped to her arm, with another tube connected to a second bag. Her hands lie limp on top of the covers, and I take one. "Brigid? It's Kira. I hope you can hear me."

Nothing. Not a flicker of response. Her freckles look dark, her skin ghostly white.

"Hey. So I don't know if anyone told you. But Laney...well, Laney is dead. She's gone, Brigid. And it turns out she was adopted. There's no one to bring you back. No blood relatives. So you have to come back on your own." I squeeze her hand and hope for something in reply.

Nothing.

"I'm so sorry I messed up. And you know how I hate random. Everything about this feels like chaos. Like out of nowhere, all this just *happened*. And I don't know if I can handle it. But I *have* to, right? So I won't give up. I'll find the way back for you." That feels like a lie. I'm already out of ideas. I need some new ones. I better change the subject.

"There's this guy, Max. He's super nice. Helpful. But the person I need is *you*, Brigid."

It's not easy to talk to someone who doesn't talk back. Doesn't matter. "Remember how we liked to try and figure out why you saw the ancestor you saw? Out of all the possibilities? And we thought maybe it was to show how their choices affect us?

Like, if they hadn't done X, then their offspring wouldn't have the same life.

"We knew emigrating was a big one. Obviously. If their grandparents had stayed in France or Pakistan or wherever? The kid's life could be so different from here in Canada." It feels like I'm babbling. But I keep going.

"Or remember when you saw that ancestor converting to Christianity? The kid was so amazed. Said they couldn't picture life without religion. They never thought about it being a choice."

A nurse enters the room, shoes squeaking. "Hello," she says. She glances at Brigid, then checks the bags of fluid. "If you don't mind," she says, "I need to check the output too."

"The output?"

The nurse nods toward the other end of the bed. "Fluids go in one way and come out another."

"Oh! Right. Well, uh, someone is waiting for me.

Maybe I should go now." I give Brigid's hand one final squeeze. "I'll try to come back tomorrow, Brigid. Every day, if I can."

The nurse smiles. "Please do. She hasn't had many visitors."

"But her mom's been here, right?"

She frowns. "Haven't seen her for a day or two."

Wow. Brigid's mom is something else. So cold. I leave the room feeling sad. I spot Max waiting down the hall. He sees me too. "Hey," he says. "How's she doing?"

I shake my head.

"Sorry to hear," he says. "Ready to go home?"

"Yeah. Thanks." But do I want to go home and sit with my thoughts? No. I need someone to talk to. I steal a sideways look at Max. "But first..." I was going to say *first, maybe we could take a walk.* Only with the damn crutches, that's not happening.

"But first?" Max prompts. "Do you need to stop at a store on the way?"

"No. It's fine."

"Would you like to go for a coffee or something?"

"Yes!" I sound a little eager. "I mean, sure. If you like."

"I could go for a coffee," he says.

Does this mean we're going on a date? No. I give myself a mental smack on the forehead. He's just being nice, is all. But why? It makes me wary. "Are you always this nice?" I ask.

He grins. "Nope. But my parents and I saw you at Laney's memorial. With those other girls. It looked like they had you cornered, and Mom said I should check. And we knew you were at the accident. Just because you're not in a coma or–dead–you still had a shock. It must be hard for you, Kira."

Max must see something in my face, because he stops walking. Puts an arm around my shoulders and gives me a quick half hug. "You're not okay, are you?"

My lower lip starts quivering, and I bite down to stop it. My throat is too tight to speak, so I just shrug.

By the time we get to his car, I've got the tears swallowed down. Max puts on the same soothing guitar music, and we don't talk until we get to the coffee shop. We get our drinks and sit outside at a little bistro table.

"Tell me about Brigid," he says.

"Brigid." What should I say? "Okay. She lives with her mom, and she's an only child. Like me. Maybe that's part of it—our friendship, I mean. We became like sisters. Close. And her mother..." My shoulders rise as I try to find words. "I'll just say she's not the best. She's super religious. Which isn't bad, except she's all about sinning and hell and the devil. She never talks about love. It's really harsh."

"Oh man. That's too bad." He waits a beat, then asks, "What about this thing Brigid does? Past-life readings."

"Not past lives like reincarnation. She sees ancestors. Weird, I know. But that's how it works."

"Sounds cool," he says. "Did she ever tell you about your ancestors?"

"No."

"Why not?" he asks.

I use my straw to stir my drink. "I tried once. But I couldn't go through with it. Some people don't feel the readings at all. But others, like me? It's hard to describe. It felt invasive. There was this instant vibration, and every nerve in my body was buzzing. Or burning. Anyway, I stopped before she even got started."

Max's brows go up, and he whistles. "Sounds sorta creepy. So what sorts of things has she seen?"

"You name it. She's seen soldiers with PTSD—they called it shell shock back then. A woman dying in childbirth. Another time she saw a woman who'd adopted her nephew. He'd been bitten in the face by a rabid dog, and the doctors back then treated it with acid."

"Say what?"

"I know, right? So anyway, this kid was badly scarred, and he wouldn't come out of the basement. He just hid down there. An aunt and uncle came to visit, and they knew doctors in the east who could help him. So they took him home with them, and the doctors did help. He was left with only one scar and went on to have a good life."

"Wow. That's incredible." A sad look passes over his face. "I wish Laney had heard about her ancestors before..." His hand clenches into a fist.

Softly I say, "Tell me about Laney."

Sadness mists his eyes. He sighs. "She was great. Fun-loving, you know? But there was always this little piece of her that seemed sort of lost. Like she was looking for a way to connect the dots. We were close, even though she was a few years younger than me. I felt sort of protective toward her."

He seems like that sort of guy. Protective. Safe.

Safe enough to tell him the whole truth about Brigid? That she can't come back unless we find Laney's blood relative?

Chapter Eight

I don't tell Max the whole truth. I'm the one who needs to figure this out. But as the days drag by, I feel more hopeless. I go daily to see Brigid, and only once do I see her mom there. Mrs. Moore is standing over Brigid's bed, staring at her. She looks angry—or something like that. When I greet her, she just gives me a look and leaves. She's never liked me, but Brigid said I shouldn't take it personally—her mom doesn't like anyone.

Every idea I get to track Laney's relatives is a dead end. The only possibility left is that her adoptive parents know something. But if they do, they never told Laney, so why would they tell me?

I'm so lonely. The thought creeps in that Brigid may never come back. Never. I'll head into twelfth grade without a single friend. Not a real one. The few kids that bothered to check in with me after the accident have stopped. They were probably just nosy.

The only bright spots in my days are the messages from Max. Just stuff like ***How are you? Any change in Brigid?*** He sends a photo of Laney and says he misses her. After that he sends a photo of a dragonfly nymph, a baby. Then he tells me they breathe through their butts.

I laugh and realize I haven't heard myself laugh for a long time.

Can we go for coffee? I reply.

I thought you'd never ask.

I smile again. **When is good for you?**

Tonight?

For sure.

It's only lunchtime, so I've got the whole afternoon to kill. I decide I could try to look good for tonight. Give myself a spa day? That thought makes me feel guilty. Brigid and I loved having spa days. We'd do pedicures, oil treatments on our hair, stuff like that.

How can I think about pampering myself when my best friend is in the hospital? I decide I can't, but I do glance in the mirror to check for zits and such. And I stop cold. I look like my mother. Not just the shape of my face or whatever. But that sad, lost look she has in her eyes? I have it too.

Mom has always been a pessimist. I don't know why. Dad teases her about it, says if she doesn't have something to worry about, she goes looking for it. She says it's best to be prepared for the worst. I worry that I might take after her. Brigid says my worrying about *that* is proof that I do.

I turn away from the mirror and head to the kitchen. Mom is there, and she says, "I was just going to try calling Brigid's mom again."

Brigid's mom picks up this time, and Mom puts it on speaker so I can hear too. Mrs. Moore says Brigid is being moved to extended care. Doctors think the coma may go on and on. They are going to do a different type of brain scan.

Mom tsks in sympathy and says, "So difficult for you. But I'm sure Brigid will wake up."

"How do you know?" Mrs. Moore spits back. "I'm starting to wonder if it's the right thing. Keeping her alive."

God. When I hear that, I yell, "What do you mean?"

And Mrs. Moore hangs up.

Mom won't look at me. "I think she's saying they might stop feeding Brigid."

"They can't do that! They wouldn't! How could they?"

"I don't know, Kira. But a woman I know made that choice for her father when he wasn't expected to recover." Mom sighs. "You could ask about it at the hospital. See if they'll tell you anything. But I think usually they only update family."

"Yeah. Her *family* that wants her to die!" I limp to my room and slam the door. Seconds later I'm out again, hobbling up and down the hall. I tell myself I need to think. What am I missing? There must be something.

Laney is the key. And maybe her parents really don't know anything about her biological parents. But maybe they do. I have to ask.

I'm better on the crutches now, so I decide to take a bus to their house. It's not easy, but I manage. The house is quiet. All the curtains are drawn shut. I knock and ring the doorbell, and no one answers. But there are two cars in the driveway—someone must be home. I go through the side gate and into the backyard. Start calling, "Hello? Hello?"

A neighbor replies from the other side of the fence. “Hello?”

“Hey.” I peer over the fence at an elderly woman. “I’m looking for Laney’s parents. But they’re not answering the door.”

“That’s because they’re not home, dear. They’ve gone away.”

“Away?” I feel my face go slack. “When will they be back?”

“Oh, not for some time. They’ve gone to stay with family for a while. Poor things.” She squints at me. “You know what happened to Laney, don’t you?”

I nod miserably. “I know. I knew her. I just need to talk to her parents.”

The woman shakes her head. “Sorry. I’m not sure when they’ll be back.”

Sorry. Everyone is so, so sorry.

Chapter Nine

Having coffee with Max, I tell him my worries about Mrs. Moore. What she said about how keeping Brigid alive might not be the right thing.

"Wow," he replies. "So there's no other family that might talk sense into Brigid's mom?"

"No. Oh. Wait..."

"Yes?" he prompts.

"Brigid does have a grandmother. But she hasn't seen her for years. She's always been a bit vague about that." I think back to a conversation we had. Brigid either couldn't or wouldn't explain what happened with her grandma. But one day last fall we took the bus to a store Brigid wanted to visit. After that we walked around for a bit, and she pointed out a house. Said her grandmother used to live there. I said we should go knock on the door, but Brigid shook her head. Got quiet and walked away fast. And I let it drop.

"Maybe you could visit this grandma," Max says, "Let her know what's going on."

I think about it. Would I recognize the house again? I don't even know the grandmother's surname. It's probably not Moore, as that was Brigid's father's name.

Max changes the subject. Tells me a funny story about how one of the kids at camp knocked him into the pond. He came up dripping with algae, so he pretended to be a swamp monster. Chased the kids around for a while.

I laugh, but maybe my voice is wistful when I say, "Sounds like the kids are happy there."

"They are. But what about you, Kira? What makes you happy?"

I shrug. "At the moment, not much. But...hmm. I like coding apps. I find it interesting."

"Yeah? What do you like about it? I mean, aside from hoping you'll write the next million-dollar one."

I roll my eyes. "I wish. I guess I like the logic of it. It's...tidy."

He fakes a shudder. "Tidy?"

"Yeah. Tidy. You know what I mean. There's a process and patterns and..." His smile distracts me, but I keep talking. "Okay, so what I really like is computer science. I want to work with artificial intelligence."

"AI? Really?" His shudder this time isn't fake.

"Well, someone needs to know how to stop the robots when they try to take over."

"Let me get this straight." Max narrows his eyes. "You want to work with AI so you can stop it?"

"Yup. I mean, don't you think it's scary? It's already everywhere and getting bigger by the minute. Don't you worry about that?"

He scratches behind his ear. "Not a whole lot. I worry more about climate change. But you're right. We do need to be careful with AI. Stephen Hawking warned us. Said it could be the best thing or the worst thing to happen to us. Or the last thing."

"Exactly. And what if someone tells the robots to stop climate change and they do the logical thing?"

"As in," Max says slowly, "they get rid of humans?" He squints at me. "You have some dark thoughts, Kira."

The next day I go to see Brigid in her new room. It's in a different wing of the hospital. It smells funny, and there are three other people in the room. Old people. So old, it's scary to look at them.

Brigid still has her feeding tube in, so that's a relief. I talk to her like always, about anything that pops into my head. The weather, my leg. School starting again in September. How she needs to wake up and go with me. That Max is great to talk to. I keep babbling, and finally a nurse comes in.

"Hey," I say. "Hi. Can I ask you something?"

He glances my way. "You can ask."

"So, speaking hypothetically, if someone is in a coma, you don't just pull the plug on them, right?"

He shrugs. "It depends."

"Right. But the thing is...the doctors wouldn't just give up, would they? Like, stop feeding someone?"

His brows scrunch together. "That's not their decision to make. Every situation is different, and it's up to the family to decide what's best."

I swallow. "Can you tell me what Brigid's mother has decided?"

"I'm afraid not." He turns away. "I need to check on my other patients. Take care."

I've been dismissed.

I return to Brigid, grab her hand, squeeze hard. "Come back, Brigid. Please! Come back now!"

Nothing.

Another nurse enters the room and comes toward us. "Hi. I'm here to do Brigid's physio."

"Physio?"

"Yes. We need to exercise her muscles each day. People lying in bed get weak, but this helps. For when she wakes up. You're welcome to stay and watch."

A wave of emotion washes through me. It's a fizzy feeling, like little clumps of lead are suddenly transformed into bubbles. Rising and floating. Hope. "So you're expecting her to wake up?"

She smiles. "Of course. She's young and healthy. She'll get there."

The other nurse calls her. "Manjit? Can I have a word?"

Manjit goes to him, and he speaks in a low voice.

I can't hear what he says, but Manjit's smile fades. She glances over at me. Nods.

"I think I'll go now," I say loudly.

I spend the rest of the day in a weird sort of frenzy. I research psychic abilities and can't find anything that sounds like Brigid's talent. I click on link after link and find myself reading about near-death experiences. That might be where Brigid is, in some sort of limbo. Or is she still with Laney's ancestors, even though Laney is gone? I can't know. I want to believe Brigid is fine wherever she is.

People who have nearly died are often brought back with CPR or some sort of shock to the heart. And then I find a different thing—shock therapy. Doctors send shock waves into the brain to treat certain mental health conditions.

Wait. What? That might work for Brigid! I mean, maybe not, but it's got to be worth a try. I hear Mom come in the door, and I grab my crutches. I want to tell her my idea. By the time I get to her, her phone is ringing, and she holds up a finger to silence me.

She picks up. “Hello, Mrs. Moore.”

Then Mom’s face pales, and she sits down abruptly. Makes a small murmur into the phone.

“What?” I hiss. “Tell me!”

“I see,” Mom says. “Thanks for letting us know.”

She ends the call and looks at me, her eyes huge. “I’m so sorry, Kira, honey.”

A gut punch of terror grips me. “Are you saying… is Brigid…?” I can’t bring myself to finish the sentence. Dead.

“No.” She shakes her head. “Not…that. But the thing is, the brain scan they did on Brigid this afternoon showed no activity. The doctors say she’s brain-dead.”

“They’re wrong! So what are they going to do? Because I have an idea.”

Mom’s look makes me stop. “Mom?”

"Mrs. Moore. In her words…she's preparing to stop the feeding tube. To 'free Brigid to go home to the Lord.'"

Chapter Ten

I spend hours curled into a ball on my bed. This is my fault. I should have been certain that Laney had a blood relative to bring Brigid back. I failed my best friend, and now she's going to die because of me. How am I going to live with this? I don't think I can.

And then I remember Brigid's grandmother. She can't bring Brigid back. But she might be able to change Mrs. Moore's mind. Buy me enough time to find Laney's relatives. It's late, but I call Max.

He picks up, his voice sleepy. "Hey. What's up?"

I tell him.

"Whoa. What? That's terrible. Her mom is just going to let her starve to death?" He's awake now. "How could somebody do that to their kid?"

"I don't know. Mrs. Moore is a bitch. And she has all the power. I have to try to find Brigid's grandmother. Maybe she can stop her." I hesitate, then ask, "Is there a chance you could come with me to her grandma's house? Help me find it?"

"You got it. I don't have to work tomorrow, so whenever you want to go."

"First thing in the morning?"

Max is there to pick me up at nine a.m. We go to the store Brigid and I visited, and then I ask him to drive down a nearby street. It's not the right one. We go down another, and I still don't find the house I remember. "It might be easier to recognize if we were walking," I say.

Max raises a brow and looks pointedly at my cast. "Let's keep driving."

And on the next street we try: "There it is!" I'm certain it's the right house. There's a little porch in front, and the house is painted bright blue with orange and white trim.

"It does stand out," Max says.

"Yeah." I take a deep breath. "Okay, let's see if she still lives there."

We walk up the short sidewalk and onto the porch. There's a window beside the door with a little sign propped up inside. *Readings by Appointment Only.*

A tremor runs through me. Readings? I ring the doorbell. It takes a moment, but the door swings open and a woman stands there. A woman who looks so much like Brigid that I gasp.

"Yes?" she says. Then she points at the sign. "I don't believe we have an appointment."

"We don't. But I'm not here about that. I need to know—you're Brigid's grandmother, aren't you?"

Her mouth opens in a round O, and she clutches the doorframe. "Brigid? Do you know my Brigid?" Her gaze roves behind us, searching. "Is she with you?"

"No. I'm her best friend, Kira. And this is Max. And I really need to talk to you. Can we come in?"

The door swings wide. "Please do. And you can call me Gwen."

We follow her inside, and she leads us down a hall to a sunny kitchen. "Have a seat," she says.

We sit at the table, and Gwen simply looks at me, waiting. The words rush out—the accident, Brigid's coma, no brain activity, her mom stopping the feeding tube. Gwen sits perfectly still, listening to every word.

And when I'm done, her hand shoots across the table to grip my arm. "Brigid isn't in a coma," she says.

The relief that floods my body is dizzying, and I squeak, "You know!"

"Um, what?" Max mutters.

Gwen looks at him. "Brigid is trapped in the past."

Max squints at her. "Sorry. I don't get it."

"That's neither here nor there at the moment," Gwen says. "The important thing just now is to make sure Brigid is allowed to live."

"Why haven't you been there for her?" I blurt.

She sighs. "Not my doing. It's her mother. After Claire's husband died, she joined a church. Said it gave her comfort. But before long she began to say that I was a servant of Satan. Evil. Not someone she wanted around her child." She stops, her gaze distant.

"So she just...ditched you?"

"Not all at once," Gwen replies. "Claire allowed some visits when Brigid was small. But then something in her twisted. She said her eyes had been opened, and she never wanted to see me again. I tried visiting, but she made an awful scene. Acted like I was there to hurt them. It terrified Brigid, so of course I left.

Then Claire moved house, changed her number." She sighs. "And that was that."

"Wow," I say. "That's horrible. She thought you were evil for doing readings?"

"Exactly. And I did consider stopping. But it would have meant denying a special part of me. A gift. One that shouldn't be cast away."

"That's how Brigid feels about it too." I shake my head. "Do you think Mrs.—Claire—will listen to you now?"

Gwen's mouth thins into a grim line. "I can try. Tell me, does Claire know about Brigid's gift?"

"No. Brigid didn't want her to know."

Max says, "I'm confused."

I give him a quick smile. "Sorry, Max. Long story short, when Laney died, Brigid couldn't come back from the reading. She's trapped in Laney's past."

His eyes widen. "No way."

"Way. The only chance we've got to bring Brigid

back is to find someone from Laney's biological family. Unless..." I turn to Gwen. "You know of another way?"

"I wish I did," she replies.

"Wait," Max says. "Hold on. Are you telling me—no. It's not possible. It doesn't make sense."

"No, it doesn't," Gwen says. "But that's the way of it. It will take some years before Brigid can come back on her own. Even I still struggle to do it."

Max's face remains doubtful.

"Would you like me to show you how it works?" Gwen asks.

"Um. Yeah," he says. "Sure."

"I can do that. But first I need to speak to Brigid's mom." She looks at me. "Do you have her cell number?"

I give it to her, and she goes into another room to make the call. Max and I wait in silence. We hear her speak briefly, and then she returns. "What did she say?" I ask.

"She refused to discuss it." Her voice catches. "Said it was none of my business." She passes a hand over her forehead. "I need to see Brigid. Now."

"Can we give you a ride?" Max says.

"No thank you. I'd prefer to go on my own." She pauses. "But if you two wouldn't mind, could you come back to see me again later today? Around three?"

I look at Max and he nods.

Chapter Eleven

Back in Max's car, I feel...what? Happy to have found Gwen. Gutted that it doesn't seem like it will make a difference. "Can you believe Brigid's mom?"

"She sounds crazy." Max hesitates, hand poised to start the engine. "But you know what? I think you could use a break from all this. Want to hang out at the beach for a while?"

Yeah, I do. Max flashes his amazing smile and takes us to a nearby beach. The moment I step out of the car and catch a whiff of fresh, briny air, I feel better. We make our way to a log and sit. There are people lounging on blankets, others gliding on paddleboards, kids running and digging in the sand. But I focus on the waves. Tune my ears to their sound. Lean against Max.

He puts an arm around me, and we stay like that for a while. Quiet. Until my stomach gets awkward by rumbling like a pit bull on steroids.

Max laughs. "Hungry?"

The heat in my cheeks isn't from the sun. "Kind of hard to deny it."

"I can grab us something from that food truck. They have decent tacos."

"Sounds perfect." I watch him go and think *he's* perfect.

I've never had a boyfriend. Never even wanted one before. The few dates I've gone on in the past were meh. But maybe that is about to change?

He returns with the tacos and we munch, lapsing back into wave watching. I'm surprised when Max says, "Guess we better head back to Gwen's."

"Already?" And then my fears come flooding back. It's not that they ever left, but somehow, being outside, watching the waves, feeling the sun? Those fears drifted at a distance. We return to find Gwen pacing on her front porch.

"There you are," she says. "Come on. Come in. Let's do that reading, then put our heads together. I need to know everything you know about that poor girl Laney."

But once we're inside, Max gets nervous. "Maybe you could demonstrate on Kira?"

Gwen shrugs and looks at me. "Would you like a reading, Kira? To convince Max that it's real?"

"*I* don't need convincing," I reply.

But Max's look is imploring. "Please, Kira. I don't know why—probably what you said about it feeling invasive? That freaks me out."

Gwen chuckles. "Brigid's technique might have been a bit rough. I can assure you, my readings are far beyond that stage."

"Really?" I look at Max's worried frown and decide I can do this for him. He's done so much for me. "Okay." And instantly my palms start sweating. I never told Max the other reason I've never wanted a reading. Some of the readings Brigid's done were hard to hear about. Ancestors aren't always wonderful, and nobody in my family ever talks about mine. Like there's some big, bad secret.

"Shall we?" Gwen asks. She extends her hand to me. I draw a deep breath and take it. And then I'm no longer in that sunny kitchen. I'm with Gwen, and it feels like I'm being pulled into a dense fog. I want to shriek, but I'm not in my body. Or am I?

And then I just know. We're in Ireland. I can see a woman, her name is Kate, and she's in a dirt-floor shack. There are four children—skinny, crying. Then, like a movie shifting to the next scene, I see Kate with her husband and kids on a ship bound for the United States. But the man dies, along with two of the kids. I see their dead faces.

Now Kate is in a city, on a busy street. She clutches her girls' hands, and someone shouts at her. "Filthy Irish!"

Kate stumbles as she runs away. She's so lost.

I feel Gwen's presence, reassuring me. Now I see Kate in a cold, drafty room. I can sense the chill on her skin. Her two daughters weaken. Kate finds work in a factory, making straw hats, for $2.50 a week. I see her count out the coins to buy bread and potatoes. Little else. Then the factory owner stands over her workbench and says he's cutting back wages. Kate flushes red and stands, tells him, "No! You can't do that!" The despair she feels when he fires her? That emotion crashes over me, and it feels like I'm drowning. The woman running the rooming house snarls, showing her rotten teeth when she hears the news. She says if Kate doesn't have the rent money on time, she and her daughters will be thrown into the street.

A man at the rooming house, a guy with greasy

hair and shifty eyes, says Kate ought to try sex work. Says she'll earn enough to support herself and the kids. Says he'll help find her customers if she gives him part of what she makes.

Kate's despair is heavier than it's ever been, has the weight of a boulder. She looks for work elsewhere. Some places have openings, but when she goes to apply, there are signs: *No Irish*. The rent money comes due and she doesn't have it. So she tells the man, okay. He gives her bright red lipstick to wear. Then he leads her to a street corner, tells her to stand there. "Hike your skirts," he says. "Show some leg." Kate shivers all over, even though it's not cold.

My mind is screaming, and once again I feel Gwen with me. Somehow hear her soothing message. "Just a little longer, Kira."

Mercifully, the scene shifts, and I see Kate's daughters are almost teens now. And the man says they ought to work the streets too. Kate refuses, but she's afraid of him. She goes to a welfare place of some kind, and finally there is kindness. The woman there says Kate should try her luck in Toronto. She even helps pay for the train tickets. Kate escapes, and she and her daughters find work cleaning houses. Not long after, I see Kate die.

And we're back in Gwen's kitchen. I can't speak. I feel shaken right down to my marrow. Gwen brings me a glass of water, and Max pats my back. The patting feels clumsy, like something he doesn't know how to do. And that makes me smile.

"Are you okay?" he asks.

"Not really." I look at Gwen. "What the hell was that?"

"That is the gift in its fullness. I don't simply tell you about your ancestors. I assume that's still where Brigid is at—telling, not showing. One day she too could be able to—" She stops. "Anyway. That poor woman we followed, she was your great-great-grandmother."

"On my mom's side, right?"

"Yes."

"Why did you show me that?" I ask.

"You must know by now. We never have the power to choose what is seen. The gift chooses. And it always reveals something the viewer can benefit from knowing."

I stare at her. "I can't see how that can help me."

"Give it time," she replies. "The answer will come. I once went so far back with someone we saw that their ancestor was the first human to have blue eyes. Essentially they were a mutant."

"And how did that help them?"

Gwen shrugs. "That person was a bigot. They expected to be shown royal ancestors or, as they put it, a pure bloodline. Seeing their ancestor treated as an outcast in their time made them rethink."

Max blurts, "I want to try it."

Gwen smiles. "We can do that. But I can only manage one reading a day. It's exhausting, going as deep as I do. By tomorrow we can do it. Because I have a feeling..." She looks at him closely.

"What?" Max asks.

"Never mind. For now, please tell me about Laney."

We tell her all we know. Max does most of the talking, and I try to listen for some clue I might have missed. When we're done, Gwen hasn't picked up on anything either. "Thank you," she says. "I'll meditate on this."

Chapter Twelve

That evening is another spent with my thoughts. There are so many pinging around in my head. Brigid. My great-great-grandmother. I ask Dad what he knows about his ancestors, and it's not much. And I get the same answer from Mom. She only knows that her grandmother, Lizzy, came from Ireland when she was a little girl. I look in our old family photo album and find a fuzzy black-and-white photo of her. And a faded one of Kate.

I stare at the photo and shudder. What a horrible

life she had! On the next page I find an old letter tucked into the album. It was written by Lizzy to my grandmother Rose. Lizzy tells Rose she's sorry she can't afford to send more money for her office course. That she's worried about her, off in another city. She warns her to beware of the curse on the women in this family.

I turn back to Lizzy's photo. I look like her. And I remember my grandmother Rose saying the women in our family are cursed. I never got what she meant. But it makes sense now. Maybe even that sadness in Mom is starting to make sense. If all the women in her family lived in hardship, maybe being unhappy was all they knew?

By comparison, I've had it good. Huh. So maybe knowing about them is like finding pieces of a puzzle. The puzzle of myself. But I don't want to be controlled by things that happened before I was even born. To be like Mom, always expecting trouble.

Still, in some ways, I already am like her. I don't like surprises. Or leaving things to chance. I like things to be predictable. Understood.

So I use apps to identify unknown things. I wrote the Brigid app to track her readings, not only dates and contacts. I included notes on the readings—how long they lasted, what was revealed. I thought it would help Brigid to have the data, but she was never all that interested. Maybe I didn't do that to help her. Maybe it was more because her talent is mysterious, and I needed a way to contain it. Is this why I'm planning to prepare for a future where robots are taking over? I don't think I've inherited any lingering trauma. But what about the ripple effects of it?

I don't want to think about this anymore. Instead I think about all the days Brigid and I walked in the sun, or the rain, free and laughing. We were happy. I miss her so much! I never even visited her today. I promise myself I'll go tomorrow. *Every* day. Because if her mom has the feeding tube removed, how long will it take Brigid to starve to death? I can't bring myself to research that.

Max and I are back at Gwen's, sitting again at her kitchen table. She makes mint tea and sets out a plate of cookies. Says she's made inquiries about grandparents' rights. But it sounds like a long legal process with no guarantee of success. "I should have done that years ago. But I never thought Claire would cut me off for good. And I thought Brigid would come to me when she was ready."

She sighs and looks at Max. "But there is something about you..."

Max's eyes crinkle with worry. "What do you mean?"

"I'm not sure. But I've got an inkling." She smiles. "Sorry if that sounds strange. It doesn't happen often, but sometimes I sense secrets are lurking."

"Secrets?" Max echoes.

"I think you have one. Even though you may not be aware of it." Gwen extends her hand to Max. "Ready?"

He swallows hard. Then he takes her hand. I watch as *both* fall into a trance. I panic as I remember I didn't get Max's parents' number. Just in case. But Gwen said something about not needing any help coming out of the trance anymore, so I simply watch.

Max's trance looks more like someone dreaming. Emotions show in flashes on his face. His eyes are closed, but his mouth opens in surprise. Maybe even shock. What is he seeing? Then his lips press together and his brow scrunches, like he's confused. And then they're back. Max's face flushes red, and he stands. "What. The actual. Fu...!" He stares at Gwen, and then his eyes flash to me. His voice is a whisper as he says, "My father was a cheater. He even got another woman pregnant!"

"What?" I blink at him. "That's..."

"Yeah!" Max's face is red. "And she had the baby!"

"So you have a sibling you've never met?"

"I have met her, Kira! *Laney was my sister!*"

"What?" I don't understand. "What are you saying?"

He slumps back into his chair. Swipes a hand over his brow. Shoves the hand into his hair. His hair sticks out when his hand falls away, and he croaks, "My father..." He looks at Gwen. "Maybe you should tell it."

Gwen pats his shoulder, and the smile on her face is radiant. "Gladly."

And then the full meaning of this registers. "Wait. Laney was your *sister*!" I shriek. "As in, blood relative?"

Gwen laughs. "Yes! As in his half sister. Max and I didn't go far back in time. Only about sixteen years. That's when his father had an affair with a woman who became pregnant. She didn't want the child. Max's father confessed the affair to Max's mom, asked her if they could raise that baby. She decided she couldn't. Didn't think she'd love her properly. So they arranged for their good friends to adopt her. They'd been trying for a second child and were thrilled to have Laney."

Max stands again. "I need to have a talk with my father. How could he do this? Why didn't they tell me? She was my *sister*!"

I put a hand on his shoulder. Wait for him to look at me. Softly I say, "Yes, Max. Laney was your half sister. So it's possible that *you* could save Brigid."

His jaw drops, and his eyes go wide. "Whoa." He blinks a few times. "Really?"

"Really. Can we go now?"

We pile into Gwen's car, and no one speaks on the drive to the hospital. The air is thick with a weight of tension I've never experienced. I can hardly breathe. It feels like every muscle in my body is trembling. The drive seems to take forever. Parking too. We circle the lot three times before we give up and park down the street. Then there's the long walk to the building, the hallway that seems to go on forever.

Just outside Brigid's door, we stop. I look at Max. "Ready?"

"Ready as I'll ever be," he says. "Nothing to lose by trying, eh?"

I kiss him. It's just a quick, awkward brush on his cheek. He flushes and smiles that beautiful smile. "Let's do this."

Brigid looks different. Smaller, paler. And then I notice the feeding tube has been removed from her nose. I reach for Max's hand. Pull him forward. Place his hand over Brigid's. "Hold on," I tell him. "Just hold on."

His hand curls around Brigid's. He looks scared. "What if it doesn't work?"

"It has to."

Gwen pulls a chair over and places it beside the bed. "Sit here. It might take a while. And maybe talk to her," she adds. "Tell her who you are."

He sits and gazes at Brigid. "Hey, Brigid. I'm Max, Laney's brother. Her half brother. I hope half is good enough for you. I hear you've been hanging out with our ancestors. It would be great if you could tell me about it."

A sigh escapes Brigid's lips.

I pound Max's arm. "Keep talking!"

"Ow. Okay. Brigid, your friend is here. Kira. She can be a bit bossy. But she hasn't given up on you. And she's got me holding your hand. Last-ditch effort, Brigid. Seems like a long shot, but hey—"

Max jumps. "Her hand moved!" he says.

"Keep holding!"

He does. A look of wonder lights his face. His voice gets husky. "Wow. If this actually works, then, just. Wow. Gotta say, I didn't think it would." His eyes go wide as he says, "I felt that! A little squeeze."

"Look at her eyes," I whisper. Brigid's eyes are moving back and forth under the lids. "Brigid!" I call. "Come on!"

"Almost there, Brigid," Max says. He has both hands wrapped around hers now. He throws me a look of amazement. "Is it really happening?"

Her eyelids flutter. Open. And her eyes slowly focus on me, just inches from her face. Her lips move, but no sound emerges. She coughs. And I'm crying. I wouldn't know this except I see drops splashing down on her cheek. I reach out to wipe them away. And Brigid croaks, "Kira? Can you give me a little space?"

I don't give her space. I dive forward and wrap my arms around her.

Chapter Thirteen

There's a whirl of motion. Max whoops, and when I stop hugging Brigid, he hugs me—hard.

Gwen takes my place on Brigid's bed, and Brigid blinks at her. "Gran?"

A nurse dashes into the room. Her jaw drops and she runs away. Is back seconds later with more nurses. A doctor shows up. Then another doctor. Most of them have tears in their eyes. Someone says it's a miracle, and no one disagrees.

"What happened?" they ask us.

"She just...woke up," Max says. He sends me a quick wink. "That's it."

"True enough," Gwen adds.

Brigid is confused. "Where am I?" Her voice is a ragged whisper. "What's going on?"

"Easy," a doctor says. "You're in the hospital. Have been for a while. You were in a coma, young lady."

Her eyes seek mine. I nod.

"How long?" she asks. Then, "My throat hurts. Can I have a drink of water?"

A nurse produces a cup with a straw. "Take small sips," he says.

Brigid takes a swallow. Coughs. Takes another.

A doctor steps forward and peers at her closely. Then he glances at us. "I need to examine her. Could I ask you to wait outside for a few minutes?" His next question is directed at a nurse. "Has anyone contacted her mother?"

We go out into the hall. Max hugs me again, and I squeak, "You did it, Max."

"I guess I did." He rubs his brow and does that cute thing again, pushing his hair straight up. "I still can't believe it. This day has been something else."

It has. Part of me feels like a kite rising and flying high.

The doctor emerges from Brigid's room and says we can go back in. He's grinning when he cautions, "Don't stay too long, though. She's very weak."

"But she's okay?" I ask.

His grin widens. "So far as I can tell, she's just fine. We'll run some more tests, but her vitals are good. It's just going to take time to rebuild her strength."

Brigid is already asleep when we return. I shake her. "Brigid? Are you here?"

Her eyes flutter open. "Kira. Yeah. I'm really tired. You know how it is afterward."

She has no idea how different this afterward is. "I do know. I'll go now. But I'll be back tomorrow, okay?"

She nods, and her eyes drift closed. I don't really want to leave, but I also don't want to be there when her mom shows up. I might say something I'd regret. Gwen feels the same. Walking to her car, I still feel like my feet aren't on the ground. Like I'm floating. I do an awkward twirl around one of my crutches, and Max laughs. "That. Was. Incredible. Seriously. Did today really happen?" His grin fades as he adds, "And Laney. My sister?"

I don't want to tell him I'd forgotten that. Not totally forgotten, but now that he's reminded me, I'm not sure what to say. "I'm sorry, Max. That was a shocker."

"Yeah. A big one."

"But necessary," Gwen says.

We get into her car and Max says, "I need to talk to my dad."

He really does. We retrieve his car from Gwen's place, and he drops me off at home. I ask him to let me know how it goes. It's late that night when I get his text message. ***We talked. Going to need some time to process.***

I reply: **For sure. Do you want to tell me about it?**

Soon. Maybe tomorrow?

Anytime.

He calls the next day and says his dad is relieved that Max knows. That he wishes he'd told Max sooner. They'd planned to tell both him and Laney when she turned sixteen later this year. But he can't change the past. Max's dad said he did what he thought was best. When he asked Max what he would have done, Max didn't know.

When I go to see Brigid, I have a moment of panic when I find her still and pale in the bed. "Brigid?" I croak.

Her eyes flutter open.

"Thank God." I smile, then blurt the question that's been burning in me for weeks. "Can you forgive me?"

“For what?” she asks. “Waking me up?”

I shake my head. “For not being careful enough. Not asking people if they’re adopted. I’m so sorry, Brigid. I was so stupid.”

“Hey!” She blinks in surprise. “That’s not your fault, Kira. That’s on me. I shouldn’t have expected you to look after things for me.”

“But I wanted to. I mean, someone had to. Your mom—” I stop. I can’t tell her just how bad her mother is. Not yet.

Brigid’s eyes cloud. “Mom hasn’t been in to see me yet today. But Gran was here.”

“I like your grandmother. She’s a lot like you.”

“Yeah, I’m starting to see that. You know, I was afraid of her. I don’t know why.” She pauses. “Okay, I do know. Mom told me Gran was evil. Told me never to mention her name. So I didn’t.” Brigid’s sigh turns into a yawn.

I smile. “I think you’ll need more than a day to recover from *this* reading.”

"Yeah. It was pretty epic. I was with Laney's ancestors for a while and then...I was sort of nowhere." She yawns again. "Sorry."

"It's fine. I'll go now, let you rest." But my feet don't move. There is so much I want to talk about. I search her face. "You really don't blame me?"

A hard voice cuts in. "Blame you for what, Kira?" Mrs. Moore stands there, glaring.

"Nothing, Mom," Brigid says. "There's nothing to forgive." She smiles at me. "See you tomorrow?"

I stand. "You bet." I bare my teeth at Mrs. Moore, faking a smile. She doesn't fake one back. It's hard to walk away from Brigid, leaving her with that woman.

Chapter Fourteen

Brigid calls me that evening, her voice thick with pain. "My mother. She was going to let me die!"

It takes a beat for me to say, "I know."

"I can't even look at her. I mean, she's always been cold. But I didn't think she wanted to get rid of me."

I open my mouth to reassure her. Tell her that her mother didn't want that. But I don't know that, so I just murmur, "Hmm." Neither of us talks for a bit. We just listen to each other breathe. I wish

I could find one comforting thing to say. Finally some words come out. "You know I love you, right?"

"You might be the only one who does."

When we hang up, I go to my parents. Ask if Brigid can come to live with us. They say they'll think about it. "Please don't think too long," I say.

But the next morning, Brigid calls again. "Guess what?"

"What?"

"Gran asked me to live with her. And I said yes."

"Oh wow! That's fantastic!" I hesitate before asking, "What about your mom? Can she stop you?"

"She might try." Bitterness edges Brigid's voice. "But I won't let her." Brigid says that she and Gwen will tell her mom later that day. And they do. When her mom hears the truth about Brigid's "coma," she's furious. Says she did all she could to stop Brigid from the family "evil" and look what happened. Brigid went behind her back. And suffered the consequences.

Three days later Brigid goes home with Gwen. We chat on the phone and she says, "I'm so grateful for my gran. Getting to know her is amazing. She says that the gift of seeing ancestors has run in our family for generations. But not all of us get the talent. My mother didn't."

An awful thought occurs to me. "Brigid, if your mom knew about the talent, wouldn't she have guessed you might be in a trance?"

"She says if I hadn't hidden the truth from her, she would have known. As it was, she believed the doctors." Brigid's voice hitches. "That I was brain-dead."

I wonder if that's true. But Brigid has been hurt enough, so I just say, "I'm going to miss having you nearby."

"Me too. But I'm still going to our school for twelfth grade. I'll just take the bus. Besides,"—a teasing note enters her tone—"you've got Max now."

True, that. Max and I have become a thing. As in, he's officially my boyfriend. And what a boyfriend! He goes with me to get my cast off, and we make plans to go hiking when I'm ready. But just hanging out and talking suits me for now. He's saving all he can from his summer job to pay for tuition. He doesn't have much extra money, and neither do I. I start looking for a part-time job. My parents say after I get my license, I can borrow their car to visit Brigid. But I'll have to put gas in it.

"We should get an electric car," I tell them.

"Ha," Dad replies. "You'll need two jobs to help pay for that."

I'd like to find a job that relates to my future in computers. But the only job I can find is at a fast-food place. I take it.

Max comes with me one day to visit Brigid. She tells us, "I've been doing some research. Did you know we inherit more than just our DNA? As in, we don't just get the color of our hair and such from our ancestors. We also inherit memories."

"What?" I squint at her. "How does that work?"

"I've read about this," Max says. "DNA is the set of instructions our bodies are born with. Like hardware for a computer. But recent studies show there's more to it. If our ancestors lived through trauma, that can be passed on. It does something that affects how our genes *read* the DNA instructions. Sort of like software with a glitch." He shrugs. "Anyway, it's a cool theory."

He can be nerdy like that.

Brigid asks if he'd like to hear about Laney's reading.

His eyes widen. "Are you kidding me? Absolutely."

"You got it. I was with Laney's great-great-grandfather. He was a lovely man. As far as I can tell, it was around 1900, in Calgary. He owned a small general store."

"That's my father's side!" Max says. "He told me about his great-granddad. I think his name was Henry."

Brigid grins. "That's right. Henry. But he usually went by Hank. He was married, and they had four kids." Her smile dims as she adds, "They had five, but one died from measles." She pauses, her gaze turned inward.

"Anyway. Hank and his wife, Mary, they were so kind. He did all right with his store. Sold all sorts of things. People hung out there sometimes. Neighbors chatting. Hank knew everyone. And he knew the ones who couldn't afford food. I saw him just give food away. He'd say it was going bad when it wasn't. Or that they could pay him when they could. I'm sure he knew some of them could never pay. But he'd see a widow come in with her kids in rags—literally. Their clothes would be worn thin, even in the winter. Brrrr!"

"Didn't anyone help them?" I ask.

"Some got help. The government didn't do much in those days. There was a group of church women Mary belonged to. They put together hampers for the poor. But they could only do so much."

"Sounds harsh," Max murmurs.

"It was. But there were good times too. Hank closed the store on Sundays and stayed home with the family. Mary would make a nice dinner, and they ate around noon. Then Hank would put on some music. They had this cool old turntable. They called it a phonograph, and it had this big, fancy horn. They only had three records, and someone had to crank the handle to play them. But then they danced. And sang along." Brigid looks at Max. "You had a wonderful ancestor."

Max smiles. "Yeah. He sounds awesome. Really generous. Thanks for telling me about him."

"My pleasure," Brigid says. "And it's me who should be thanking *you* for what you did."

"Anytime," Max says.

Brigid laughs. "I hope never again."

"Brigid," I say. "What about after that? After Laney was gone? You don't remember anything from all those weeks?"

She shakes her head. "Not really. I felt Laney let go, and it was so sudden. And then everything just went dark. Like being in a deep, dreamless sleep. Or not. I can't explain it. It feels like maybe I slipped out of time."

The next time I catch the bus to visit Brigid, she asks me to go into the backyard with her. There's a big old weeping willow there that shades us from the August afternoon. Brigid runs a hand through the curtain of branches. "Isn't it gorgeous?"

"Yeah."

We sit on the grass, and Brigid leans against the trunk. "Gran told me she did a reading for you too. And she took you along."

I nod. "It was intense."

"She's going to coach me on how to do that. And to be more sensitive about how I access DNA memories."

DNA memories. All this time I've been thinking of what Brigid does as a kind of time travel. But it's even weirder than that. She travels through people's cells. That's why only someone with the same DNA can bring her back. A genetic relative. Which reminds me.

"I hope you're also learning how to get out of a reading without a relative standing by."

She smiles. "That too. For now, she's teaching me to meditate. Says it helps control thought, and that's the key."

I return the smile. "I'm so glad you've got your gran now. And I've still got you."

"Always," she says.

Always. Or at least for this lifetime. This lifetime, where I hope to spend many more hours with her. Sitting under trees. With the roots and branches and blue skies. With knowing there is so much that's hidden. Underground the trees have a vast network linking them together. And like them, we live with our hidden connections. To our pasts. To each other. To mysteries we may never understand.

And I'm okay with that. I know now I'll never be able to control everything. Random stuff happens. But I can control how I choose to look at life. And right now?

It's looking great.

Acknowledgments

Stories appear from various sources and while there may be mystery around their origins, authors don't find them complete and bound in a book without the assistance of others. For *Trance*, in particular, I must start by thanking my ancestors because (to state the obvious!) without them, neither I nor this story would exist.

I am grateful to my dear friend, Carolyn Gibbons, for inviting me to cat-sit her sweet kitty, Garbanzo (aka Gabby). Gabby's company and the hours in Carolyn's peaceful garden were the perfect retreat space for me to write the first draft of this book.

My thanks also to Roberta Martin for sharing her family story about an uncle bitten by a rabid dog and then scarred with acid; that anecdote enriched this story.

Gabrielle Prendergast, Orca editor, did a fantastic job helping me strengthen *Trance*, and I owe thanks to her, and all the wonderful team at Orca Book Publishers. They are impressively great at their jobs, producing wonderful books for readers to enjoy.

Finally, as ever, I am grateful to my critique group. For many years, authors Shelley Hrdlitschka and Diane Tullson have been here to provide insightful feedback and steadfast encouragement for my ideas. It's a joy to share this writing journey with them.

MORE GRIPPING orca soundings

When Hannah's brother disappears with their overdue rent money, she has no choice but to track him down. Along the way she meets the charming Eli, who offers to help—if Hannah can learn to trust him.

Maya is excited to hang out with her best friend's rock-star dad, but her life is thrown off-balance when he kisses her in the back of a limo.

Jake's boring day gets flipped upside down when a stranger asks him to help play a prank on her friends. But when an angry crime boss turns up at the cottage the next morning, Jake quickly realizes the night before was a big mistake, and that girl was no prankster.

Charlie feels responsible for her father's mental health. When he takes off to go canoeing at a remote lake after a period of depression, she fears the worst and goes after him.

K.L. Denman is an author of middle-grade, YA and adult fiction. Many of her titles have been nominated for literary awards, including *Me, Myself and Ike*, which was a finalist for the Governor General's Literary Award. She began her writing career as a contributor to her school newspaper but didn't take it up seriously until many years later when she found her true passion in writing fiction. She is the author of Orca Currents titles *Mirror Image* and *Agent Angus*. She lives in Delta, British Columbia.

orca soundings

For more information on all the books

in the Orca Soundings line, please visit

orcabook.com